DATE DUE

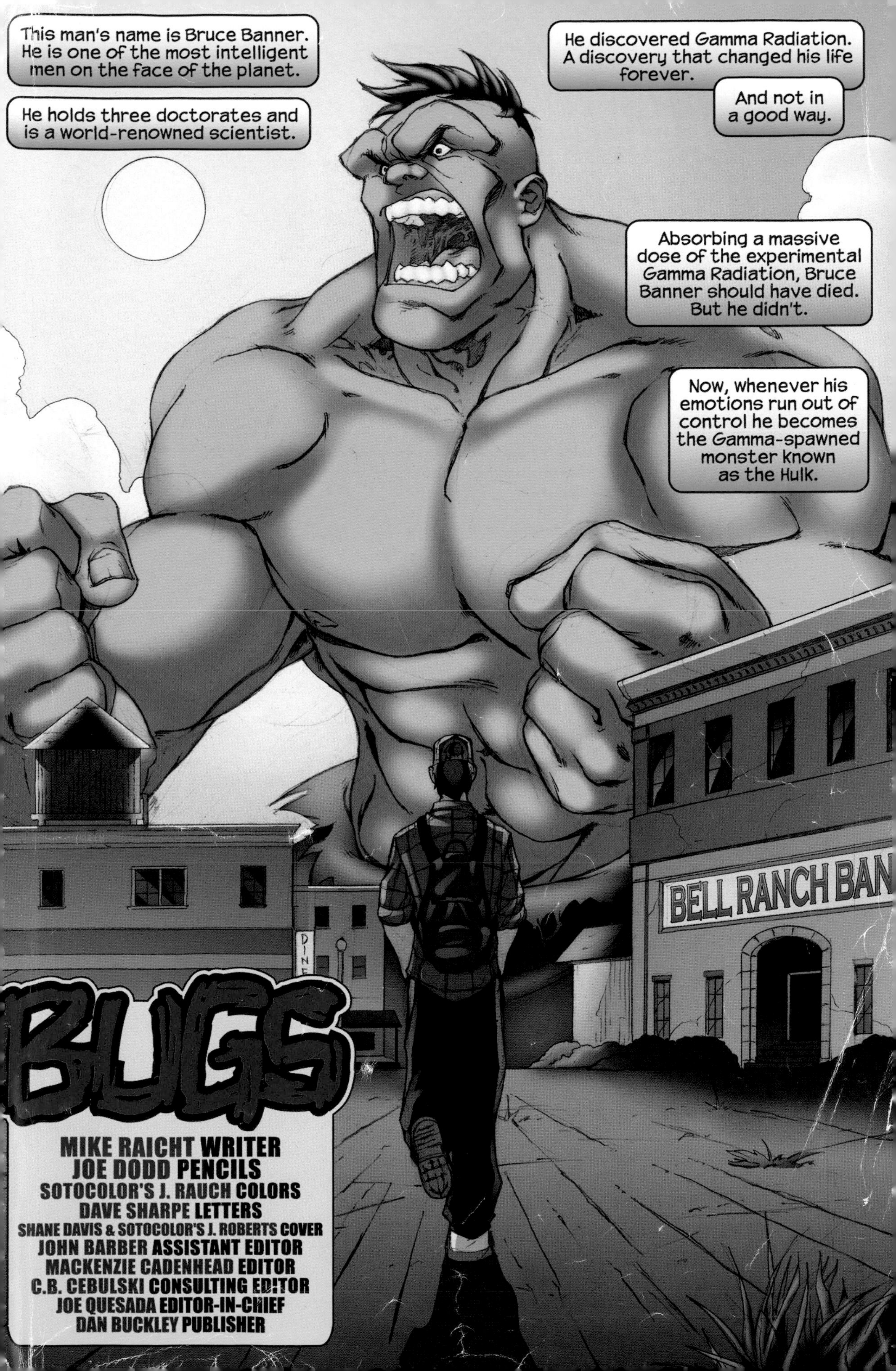

This man's name is Bruce Banner. He is one of the most intelligent men on the face of the planet.
He holds three doctorates and is a world-renowned scientist.
He discovered Gamma Radiation. A discovery that changed his life forever.
And not in a good way.
Absorbing a massive dose of the experimental Gamma Radiation, Bruce Banner should have died. But he didn't.
Now, whenever his emotions run out of control he becomes the Gamma-spawned monster known as the Hulk.
BELL RANCH BAN
BUGS
MIKE RAICHT WRITER
JOE DODD PENCILS
SOTOCOLOR'S J. RAUCH COLORS
DAVE SHARPE LETTERS
SHANE DAVIS & SOTOCOLOR'S J. ROBERTS COVER
JOHN BARBER ASSISTANT EDITOR
MACKENZIE CADENHEAD EDITOR
C.B. CEBULSKI CONSULTING EDITOR
JOE QUESADA EDITOR-IN-CHIEF
DAN BUCKLEY PUBLISHER

VISIT US AT

www.abdopub.com

Spotlight, a division of ABDO Publishing Company Inc., is the school and library distributor of the Marvel Entertainment books.

Library bound edition © 2006

Library of Congress Cataloging-in-Publication Data

Raicht, Mike.

Bugs / Mike Raicht, writer ; Joe Dodd, pencils ; J. Rauch, colors ; Dave Sharpe, letters ; Shane Davis & J. Roberts, cover.

p. cm.

"Marvel age"—Cover.

Revision of a Nov. 2004 issue of Incredible Hulk.

ISBN 1-59961-043-4

1. Graphic novels. I. Dodd, Joe (Joseph) II. Incredible Hulk (New York, N.Y. : 1999) III. Title.

PN6728.H8R33 2006

741.5'973—dc22

2005057559

All Spotlight books are reinforced library binding

and manufactured in the United States of America

Spotlight

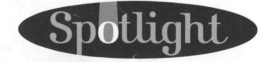

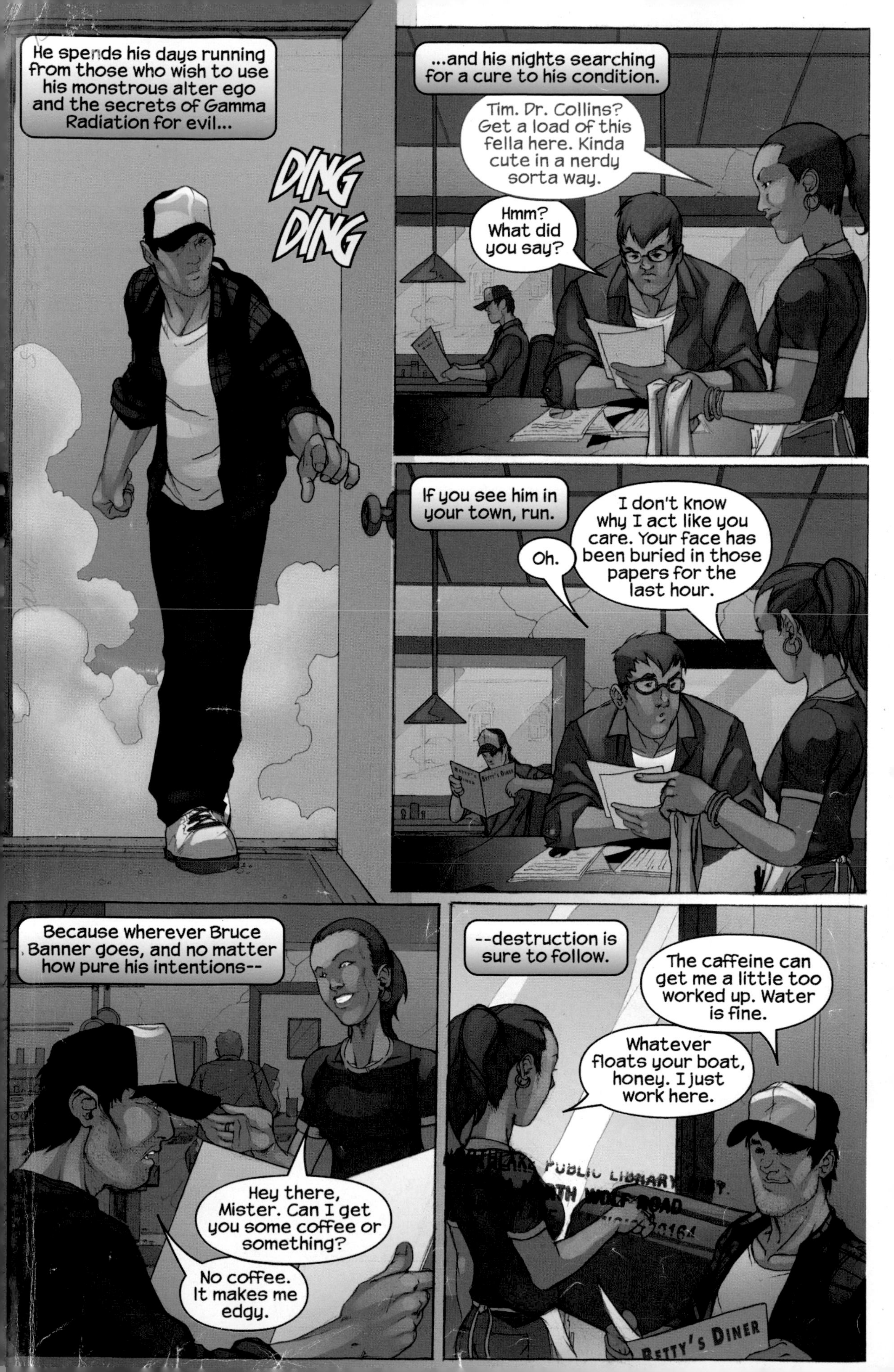
He spends his days running from those who wish to use his monstrous alter ego and the secrets of Gamma Radiation for evil...
DING DING
...and his nights searching for a cure to his condition.
Tim. Dr. Collins? Get a load of this fella here. Kinda cute in a nerdy sorta way.
Hmm? What did you say?
If you see him in your town, run.
Oh.
I don't know why I act like you care. Your face has been buried in those papers for the last hour.
Because wherever Bruce Banner goes, and no matter how pure his intentions--
Hey there, Mister. Can I get you some coffee or something?
No coffee. It makes me edgy.
--destruction is sure to follow.
The caffeine can get me a little too worked up. Water is fine.
Whatever floats your boat, honey. I just work here.
BETTY'S DINER

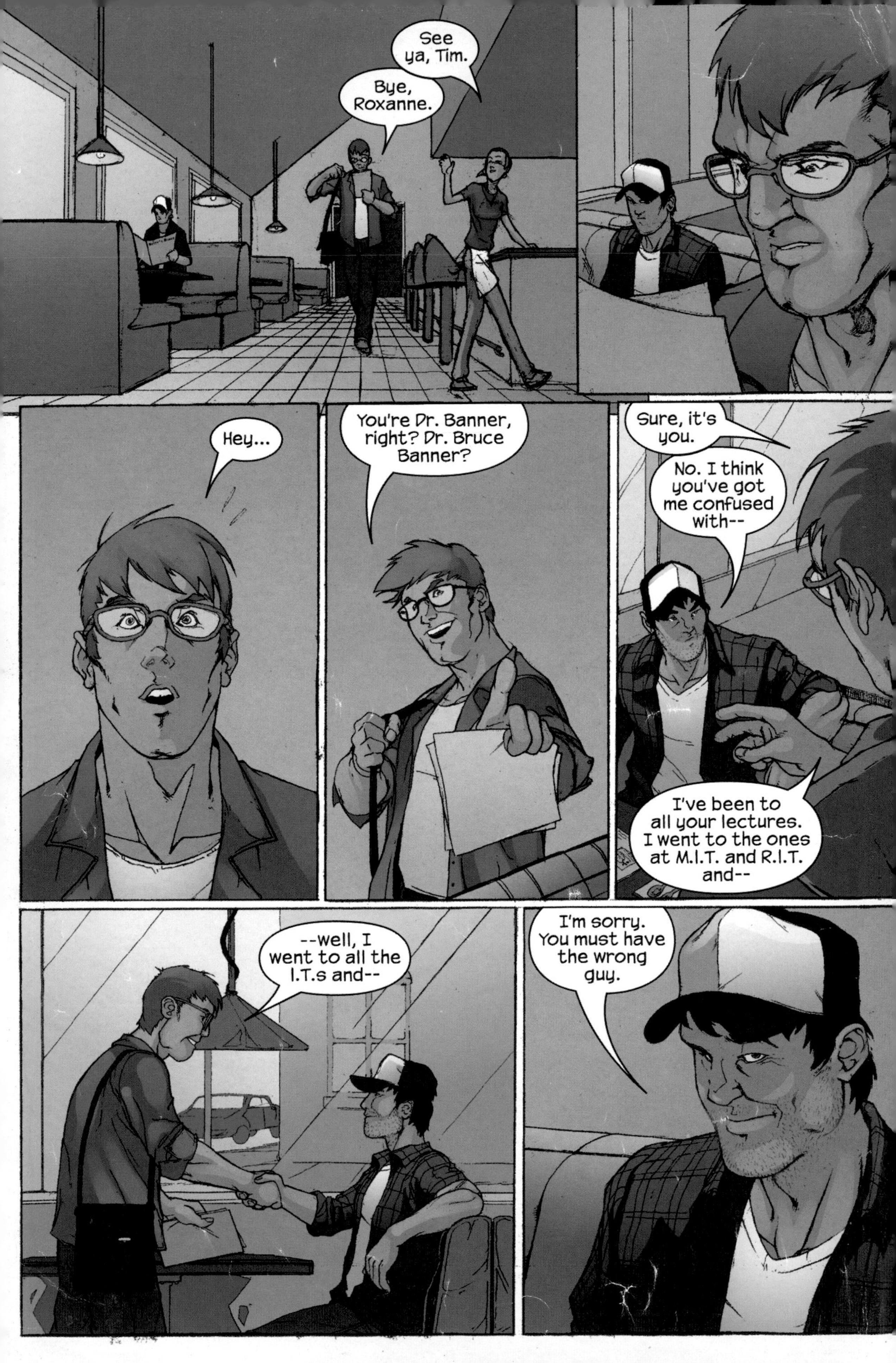
See ya, Tim.
Bye, Roxanne.
Hey...
You're Dr. Banner, right? Dr. Bruce Banner?
Sure, it's you.
No. I think you've got me confused with--
I've been to all your lectures. I went to the ones at M.I.T. and R.I.T. and--
--well, I went to all the I.T.s and--
I'm sorry. You must have the wrong guy.

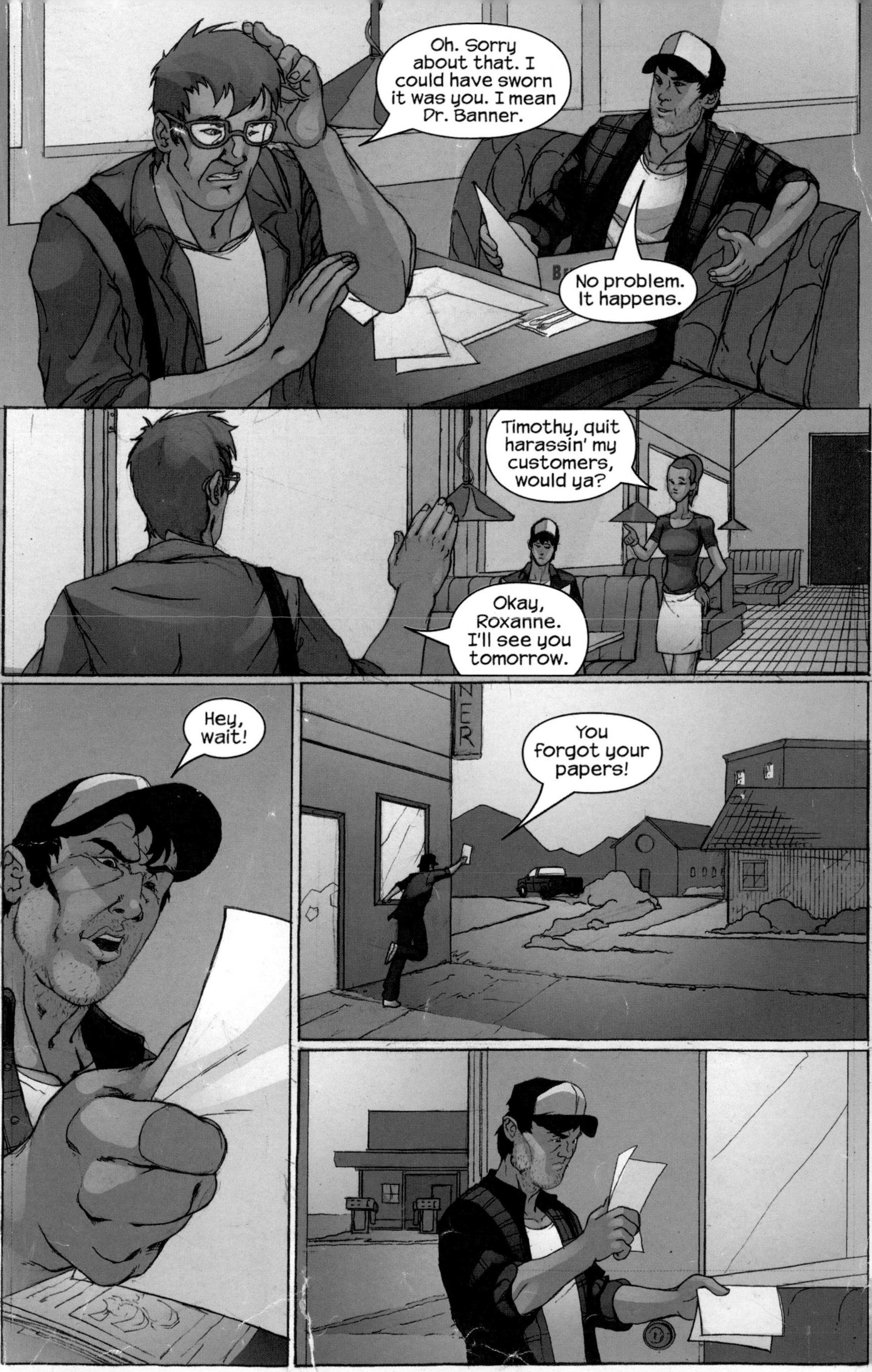
Oh. Sorry about that. I could have sworn it was you. I mean Dr. Banner.
No problem. It happens.
Timothy, quit harassin' my customers, would ya?
Okay, Roxanne. I'll see you tomorrow.
Hey, wait!
NER
You forgot your papers!

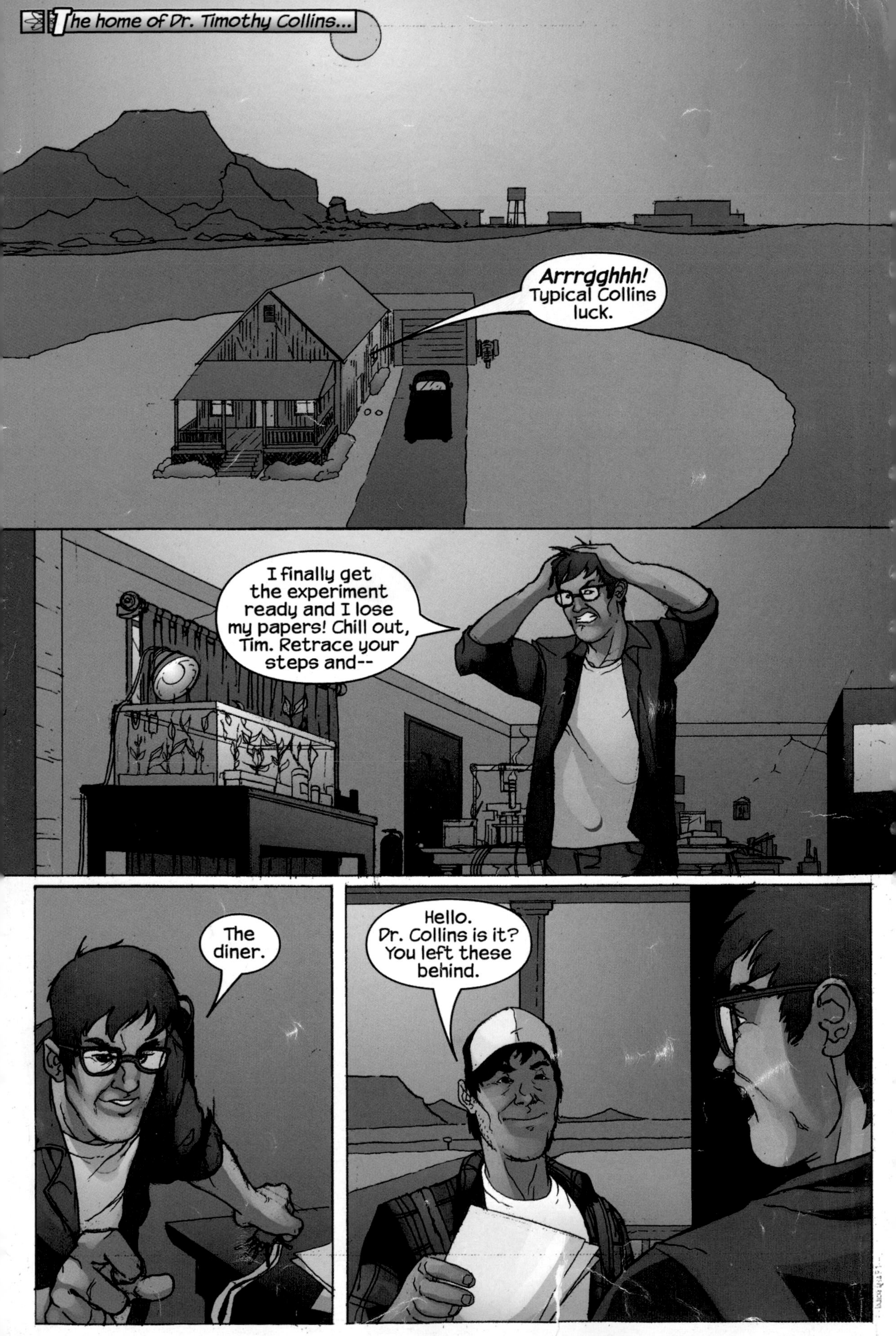
The home of Dr. Timothy Collins...
Arrrgghhh! Typical Collins luck.
I finally get the experiment ready and I lose my papers! Chill out, Tim. Retrace your steps and--
The diner.
Hello. Dr. Collins is it? You left these behind.

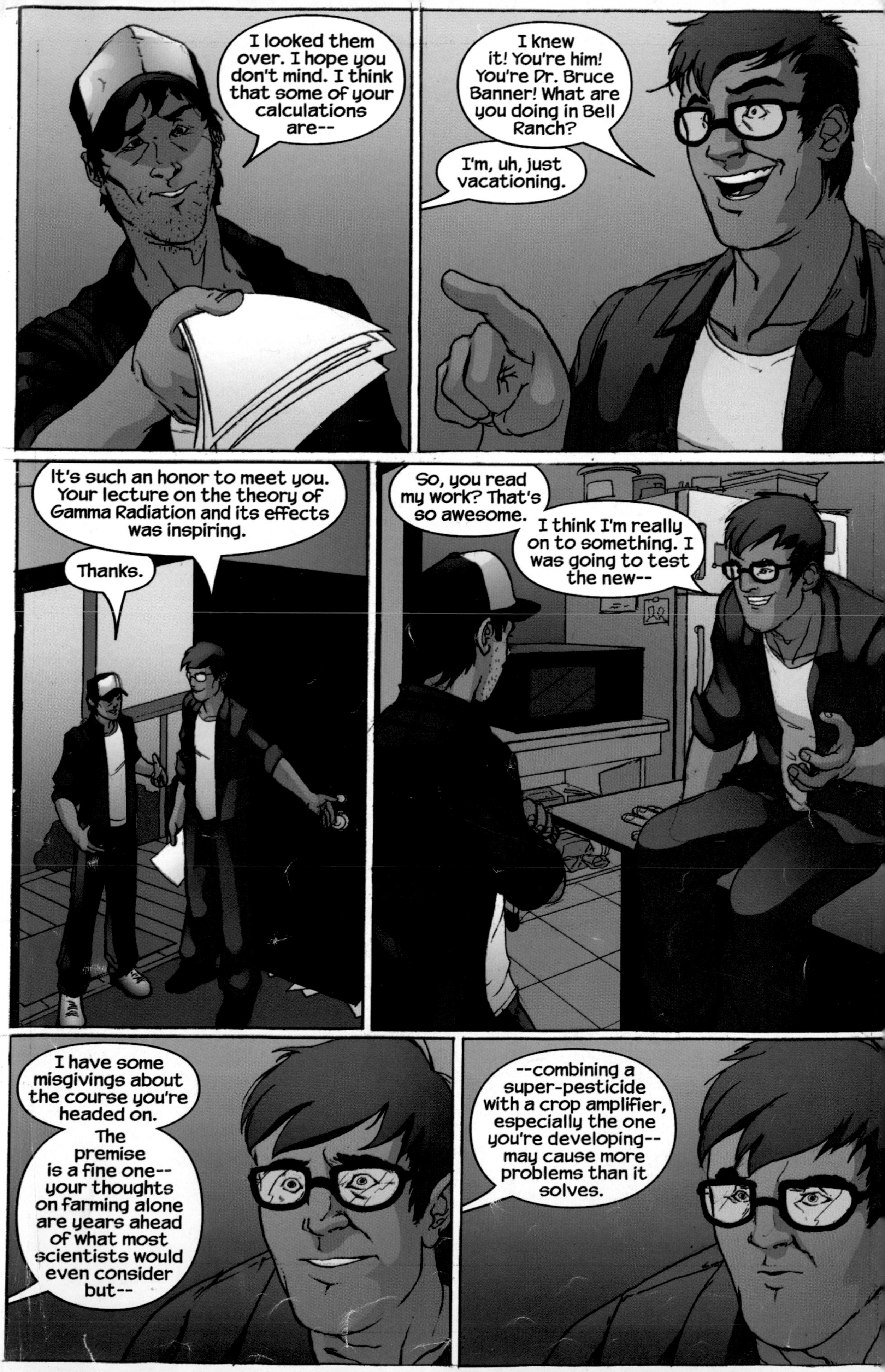
I looked them over. I hope you don't mind. I think that some of your calculations are--
I knew it! You're him! You're Dr. Bruce Banner! What are you doing in Bell Ranch?
I'm, uh, just vacationing.
It's such an honor to meet you. Your lecture on the theory of Gamma Radiation and its effects was inspiring.
Thanks.
So, you read my work? That's so awesome.
I think I'm really on to something. I was going to test the new--
I have some misgivings about the course you're headed on.
The premise is a fine one--your thoughts on farming alone are years ahead of what most scientists would even consider but--
--combining a super-pesticide with a crop amplifier, especially the one you're developing--may cause more problems than it solves.

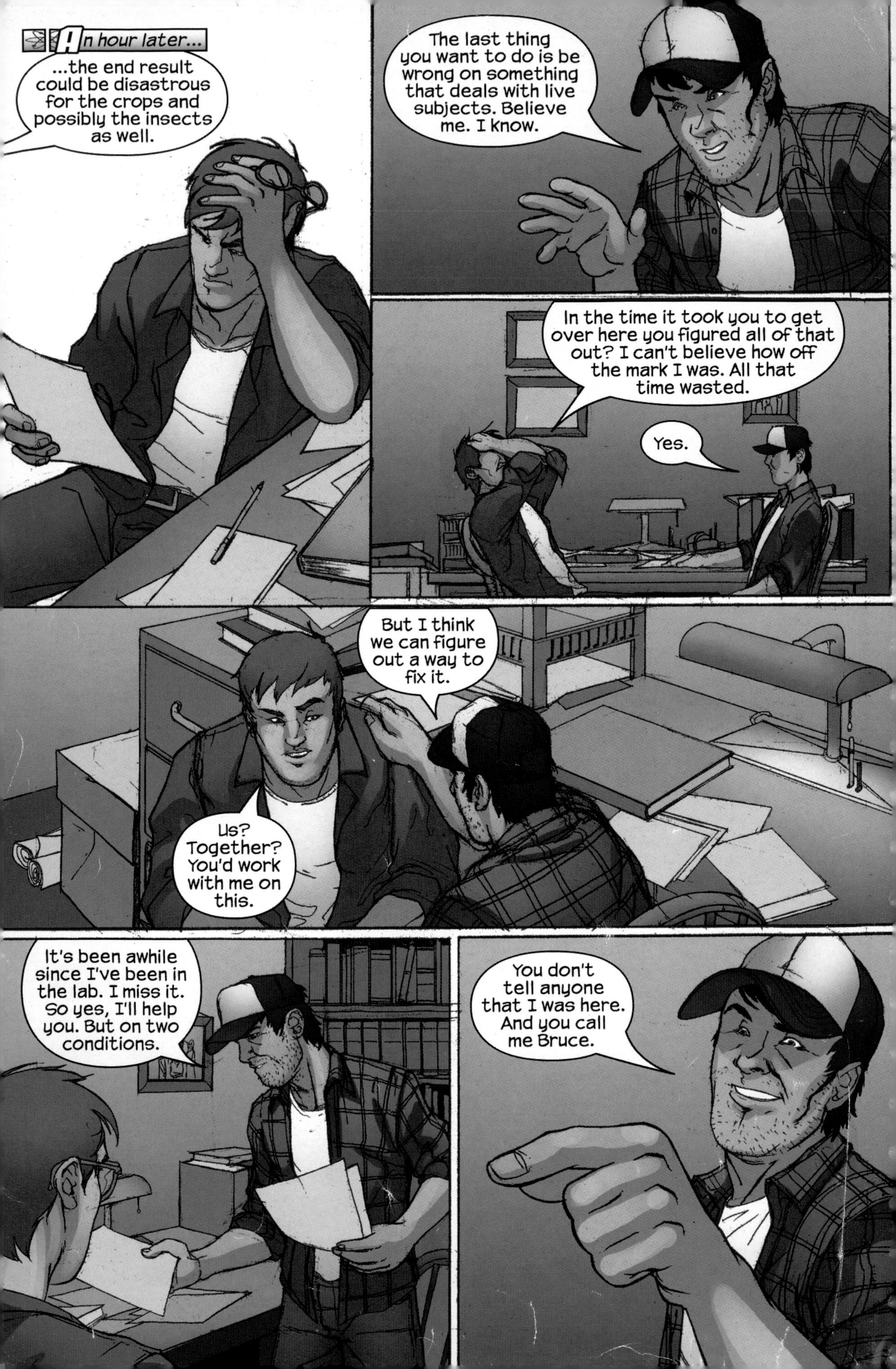
An hour later...
...the end result could be disastrous for the crops and possibly the insects as well.
The last thing you want to do is be wrong on something that deals with live subjects. Believe me. I know.
In the time it took you to get over here you figured all of that out? I can't believe how off the mark I was. All that time wasted.
Yes.
But I think we can figure out a way to fix it.
Us? Together? You'd work with me on this.
It's been awhile since I've been in the lab. I miss it. So yes, I'll help you. But on two conditions.
You don't tell anyone that I was here. And you call me Bruce.

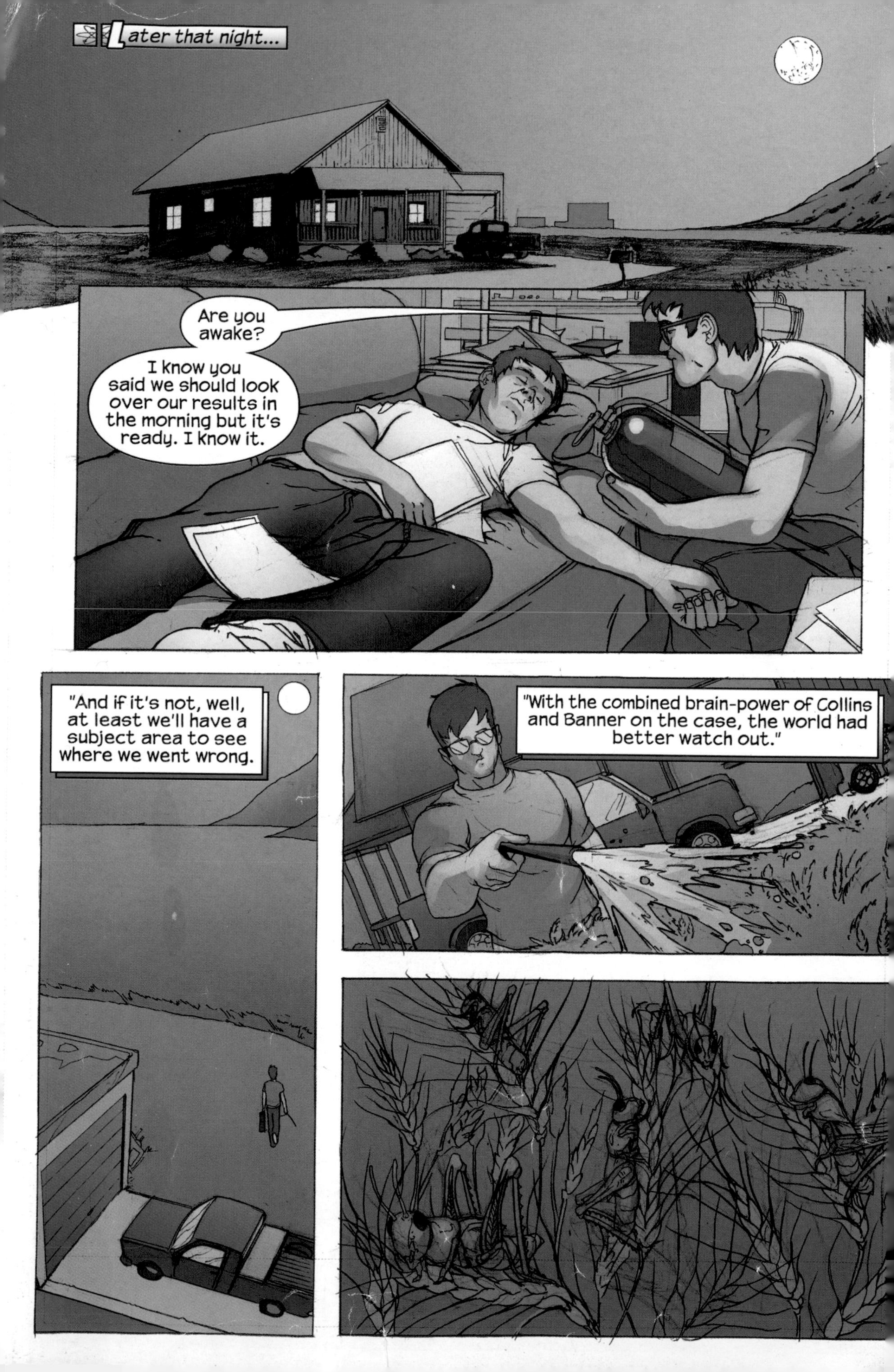
Later that night...
Are you awake?
I know you said we should look over our results in the morning but it's ready. I know it.
"And if it's not, well, at least we'll have a subject area to see where we went wrong.
"With the combined brain-power of Collins and Banner on the case, the world had better watch out."

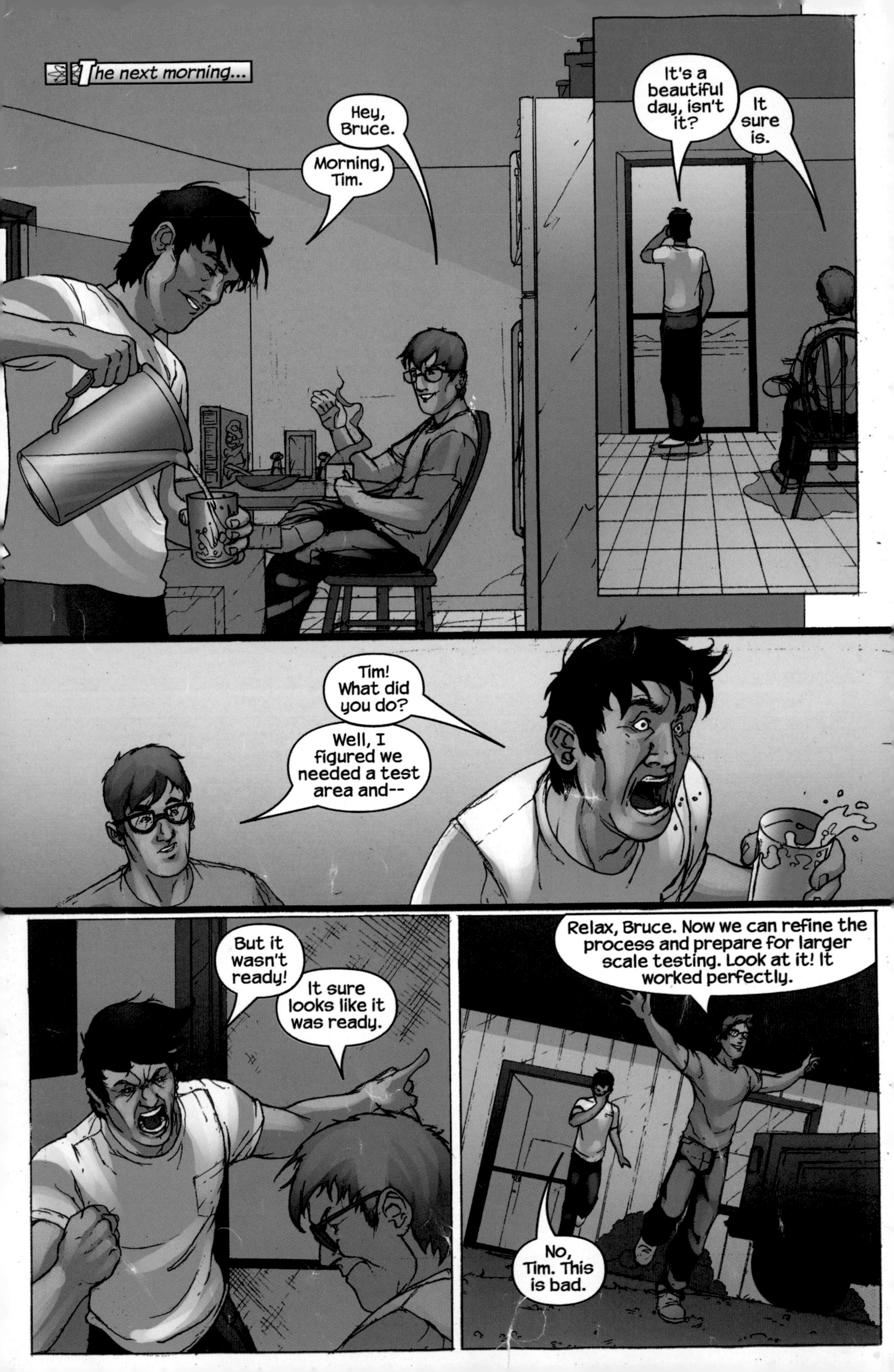
The next morning...
Hey, Bruce.
Morning, Tim.
It's a beautiful day, isn't it?
It sure is.
Tim! What did you do?
Well, I figured we needed a test area and--
But it wasn't ready!
It sure looks like it was ready.
Relax, Bruce. Now we can refine the process and prepare for larger scale testing. Look at it! It worked perfectly.
No, Tim. This is bad.

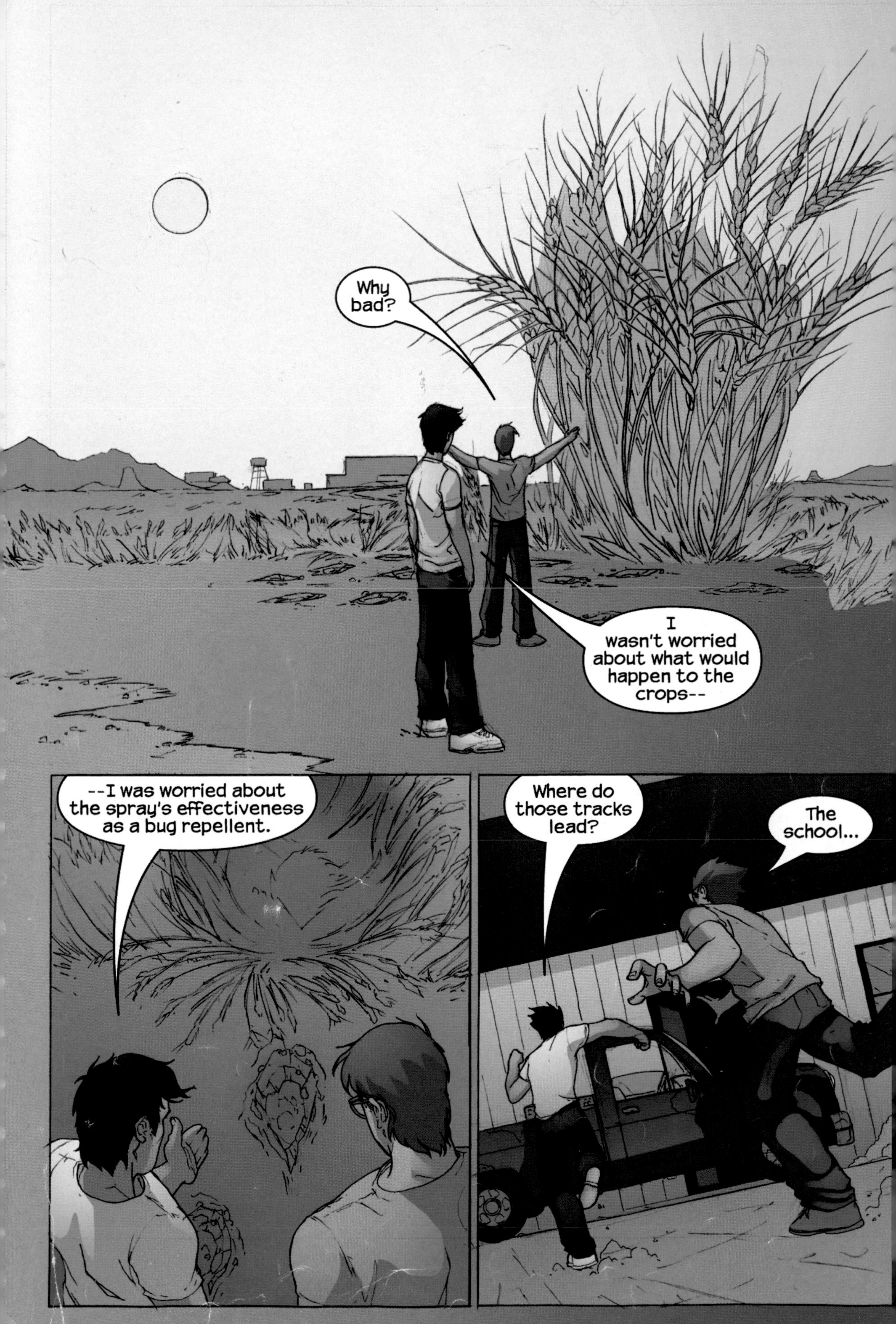
Why bad?
I wasn't worried about what would happen to the crops--
--I was worried about the spray's effectiveness as a bug repellent.
Where do those tracks lead?
The school...

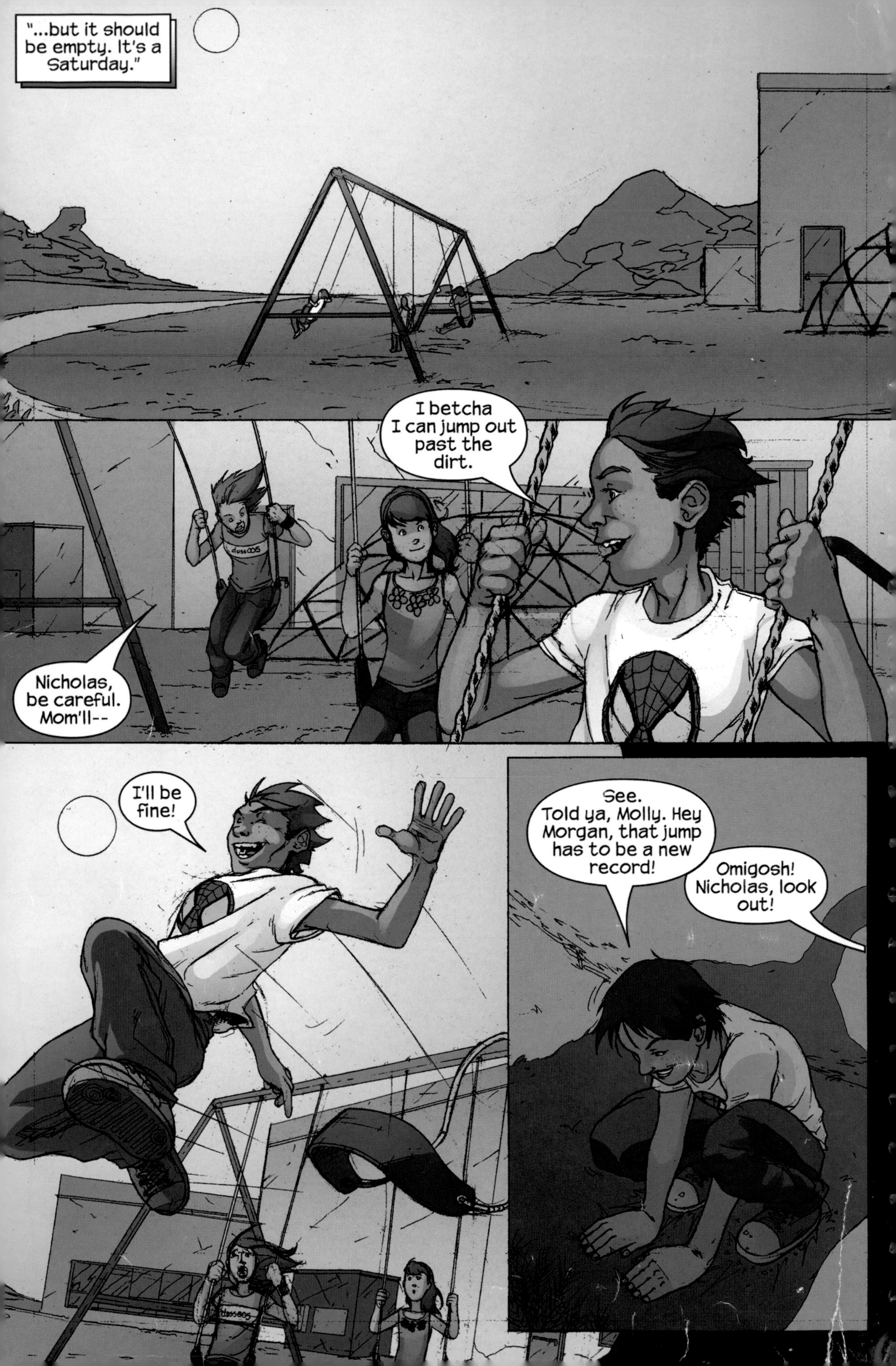
"...but it should be empty. It's a Saturday."
I betcha I can jump out past the dirt.
Nicholas, be careful. Mom'll--
I'll be fine!
See. Told ya, Molly. Hey Morgan, that jump has to be a new record!
Omigosh! Nicholas, look out!

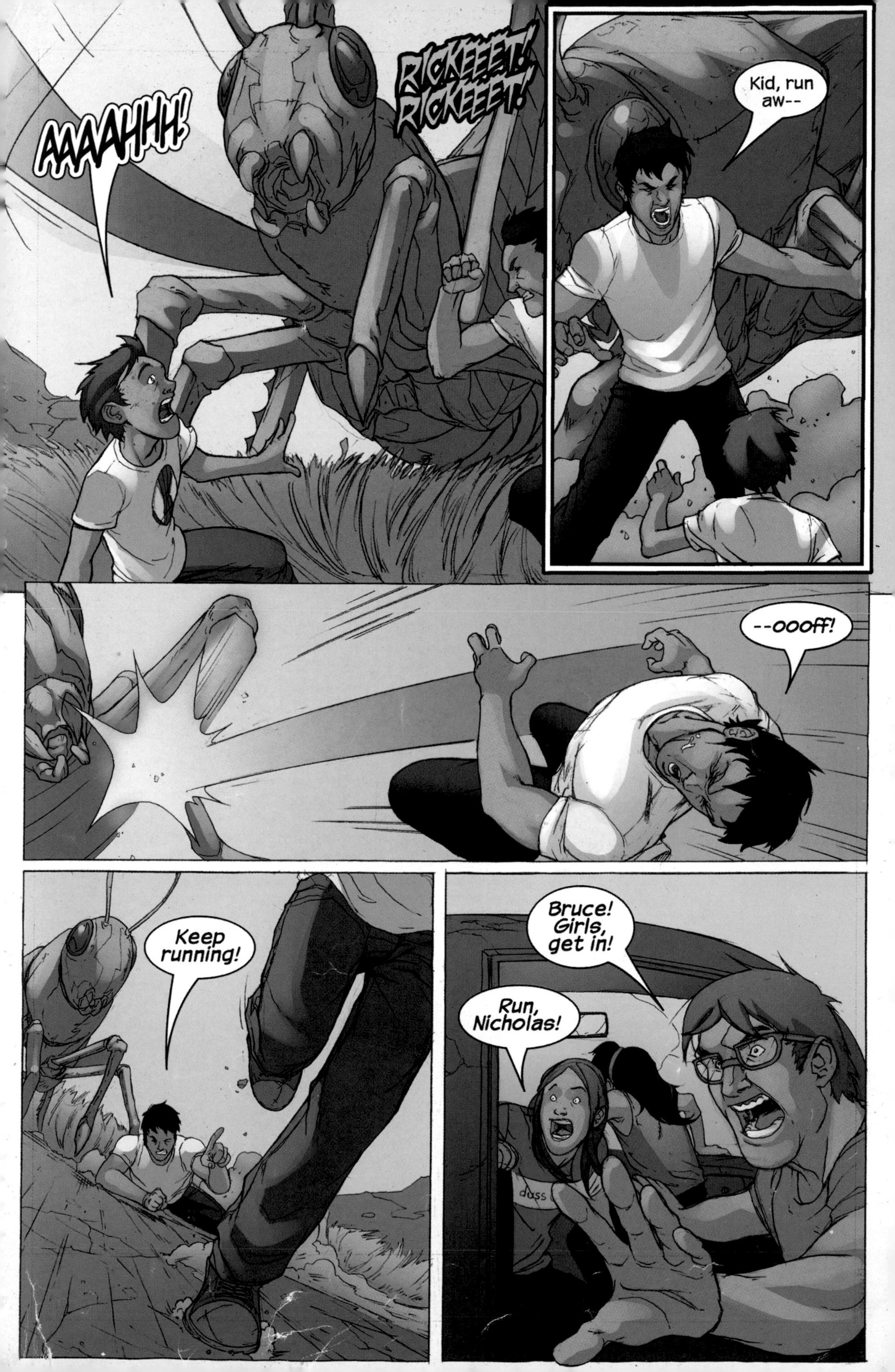
AAAAHHH!
RICKEEET! RICKEEET!
Kid, run aw--
--oooff!
Keep running!
Bruce! Girls, get in!
Run, Nicholas!

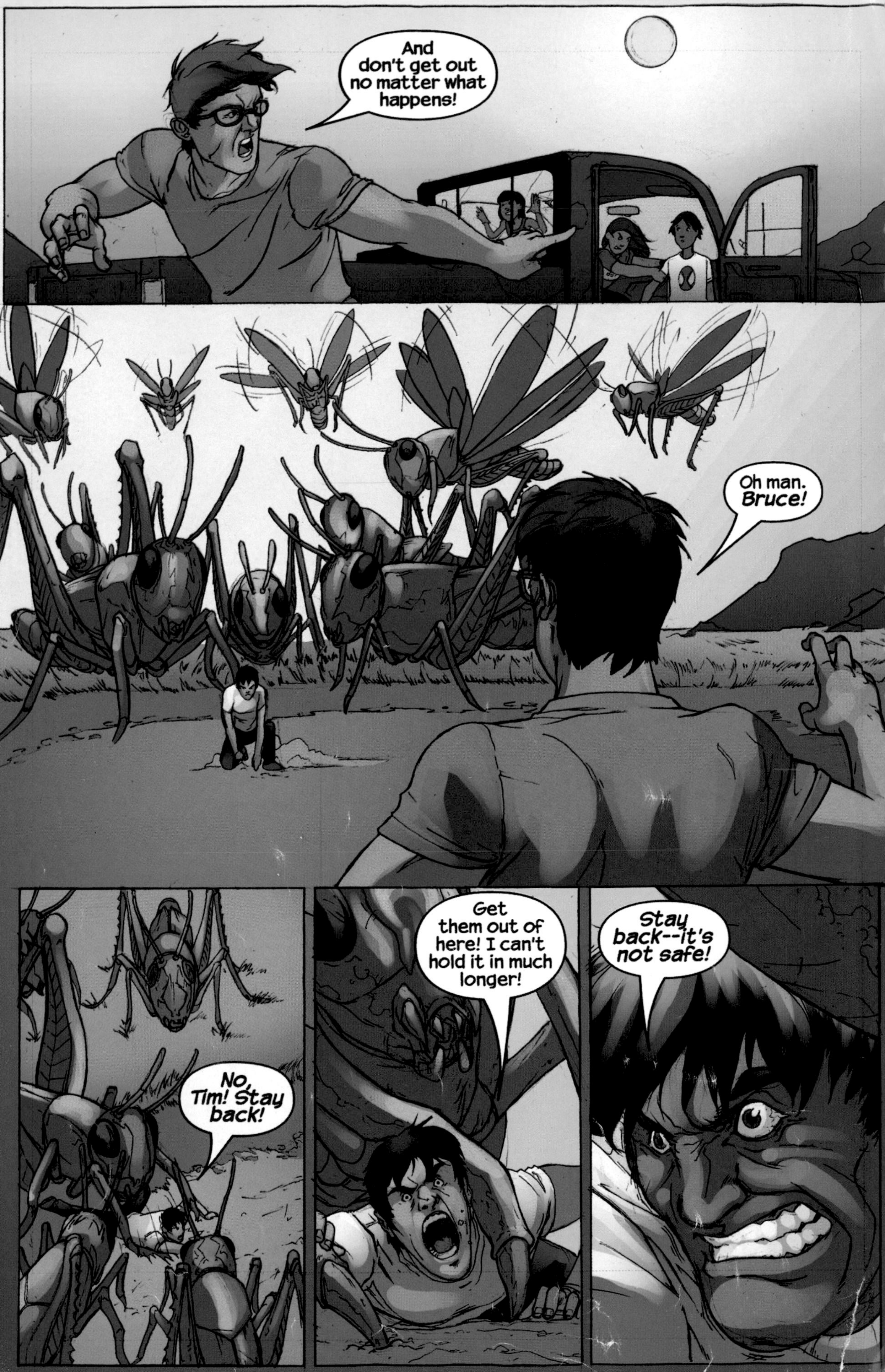
And don't get out no matter what happens!
Oh man. Bruce!
No, Tim! Stay back!
Get them out of here! I can't hold it in much longer!
Stay back--it's not safe!

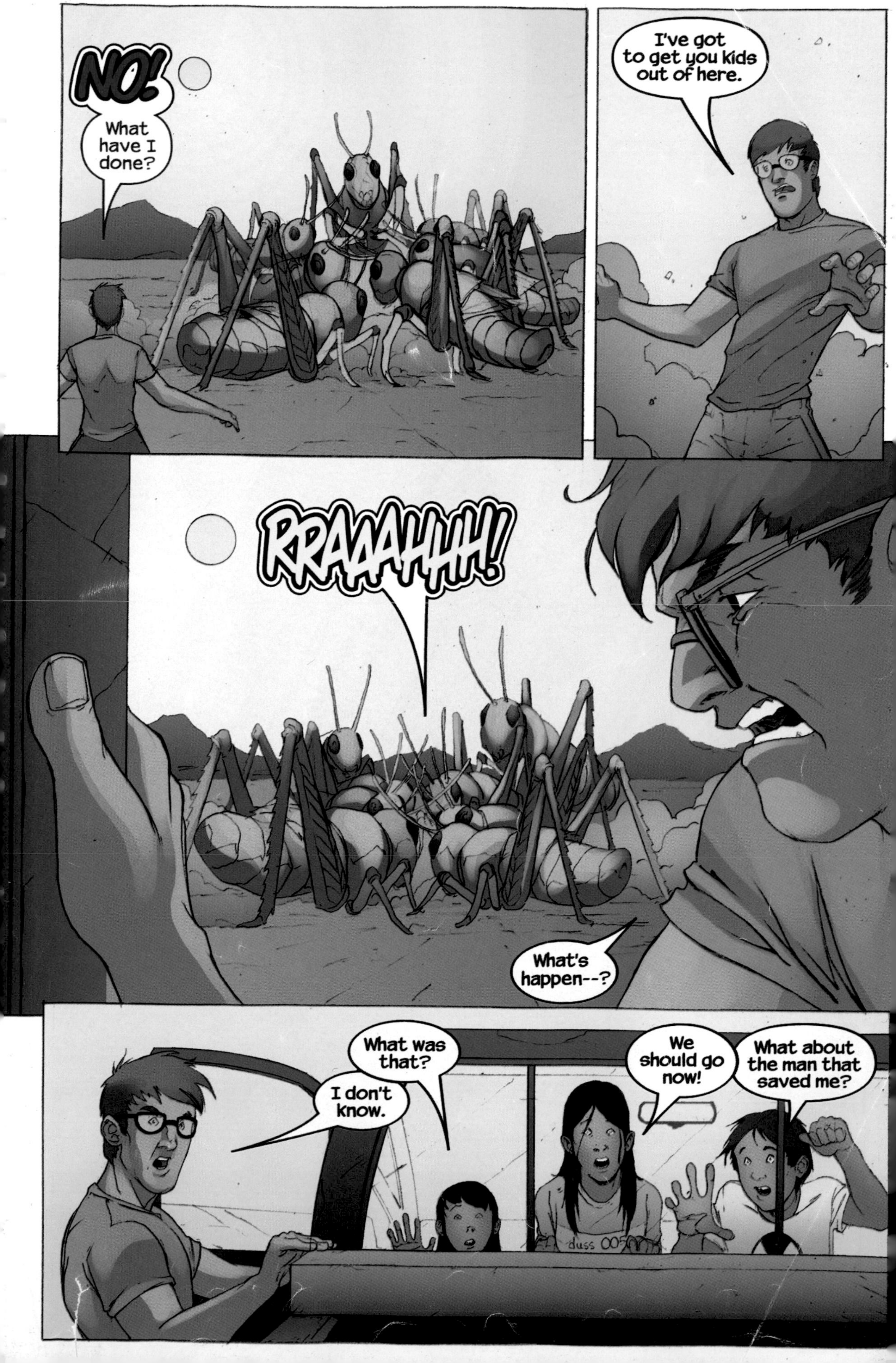
NO!
What have I done?
I've got to get you kids out of here.
RRAAAHHH!
What's happen--?
What was that?
I don't know.
We should go now!
What about the man that saved me?

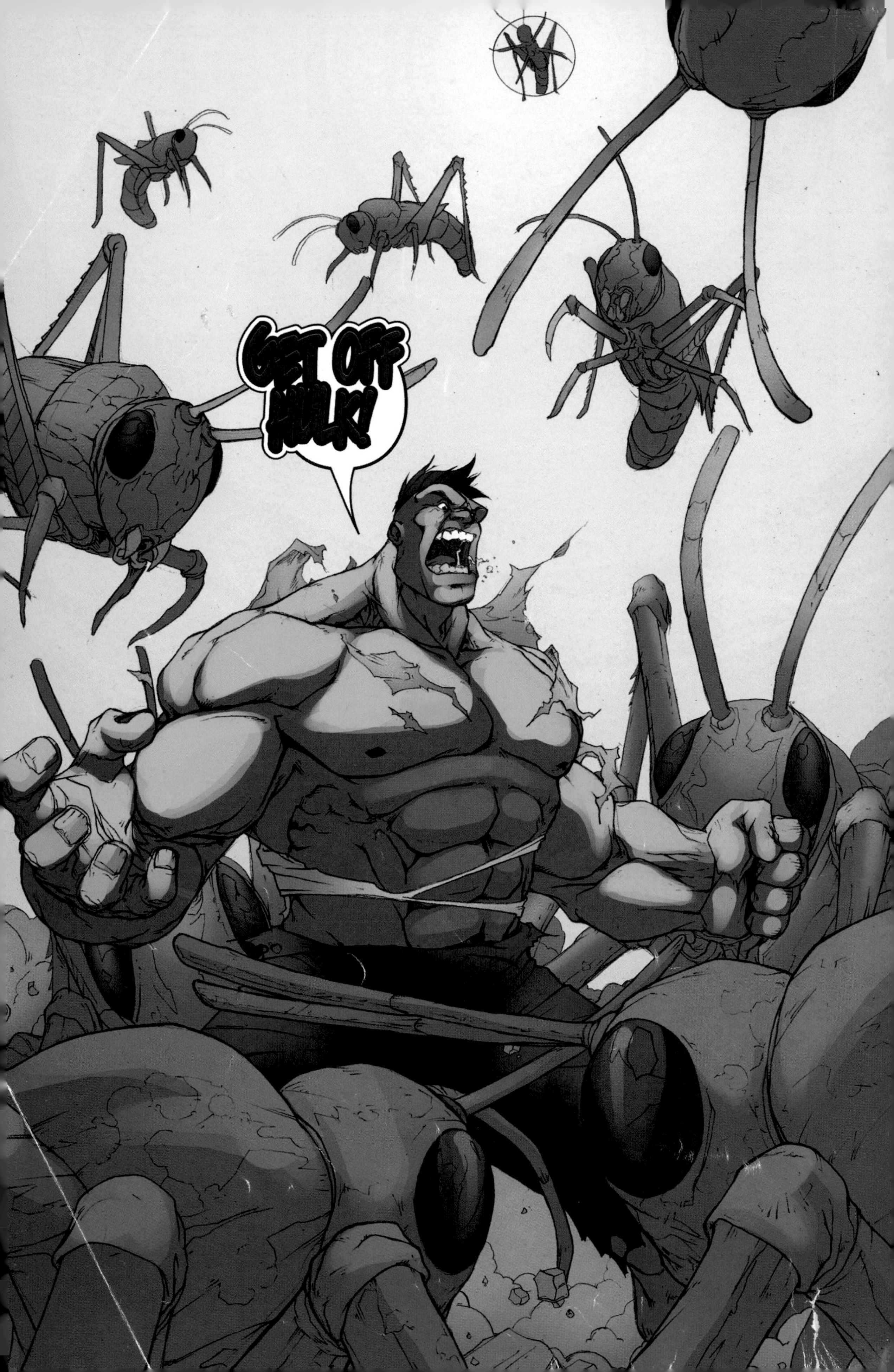
GET OFF HULK!

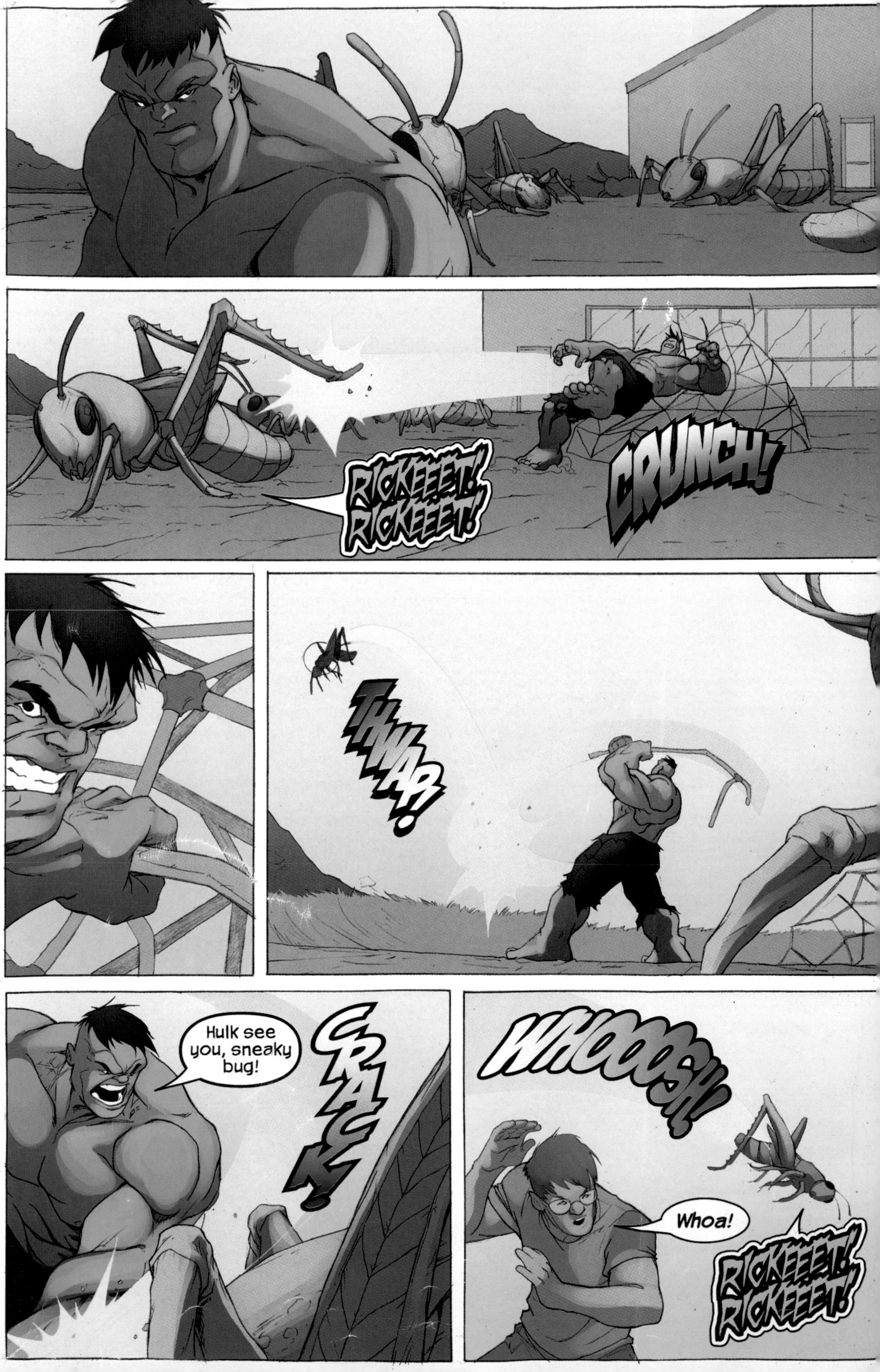
RICKEEET! RICKEEET!
CRUNCH!
THWAP!
Hulk see you, sneaky bug!
CRACK!
WHOOOSH!
Whoa!
RICKEEET! RICKEEET!

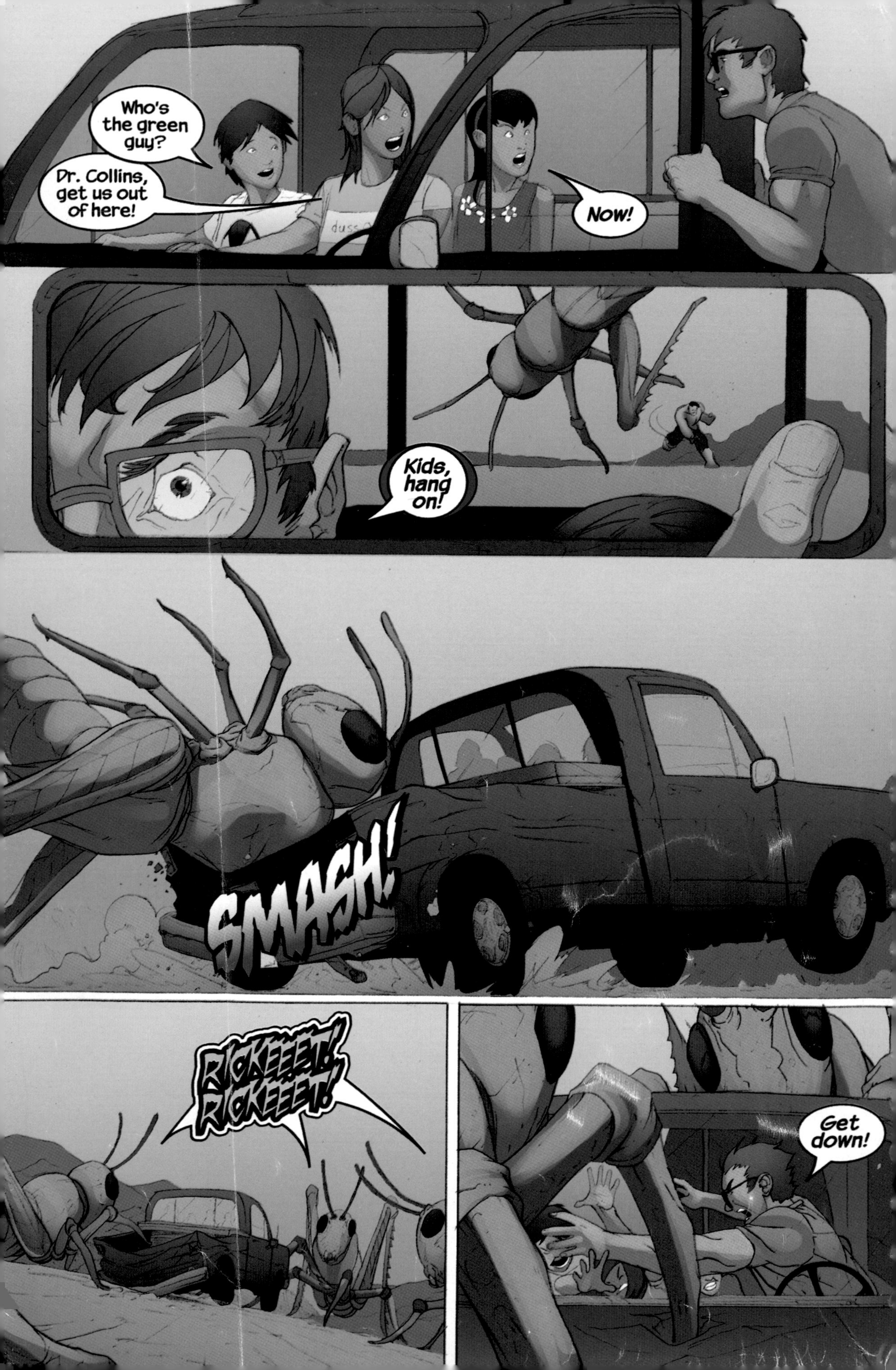
Who's the green guy?
Dr. Collins, get us out of here!
Now!
Kids, hang on!
SMASH!
RICKEEET! RICKEEET!
Get down!

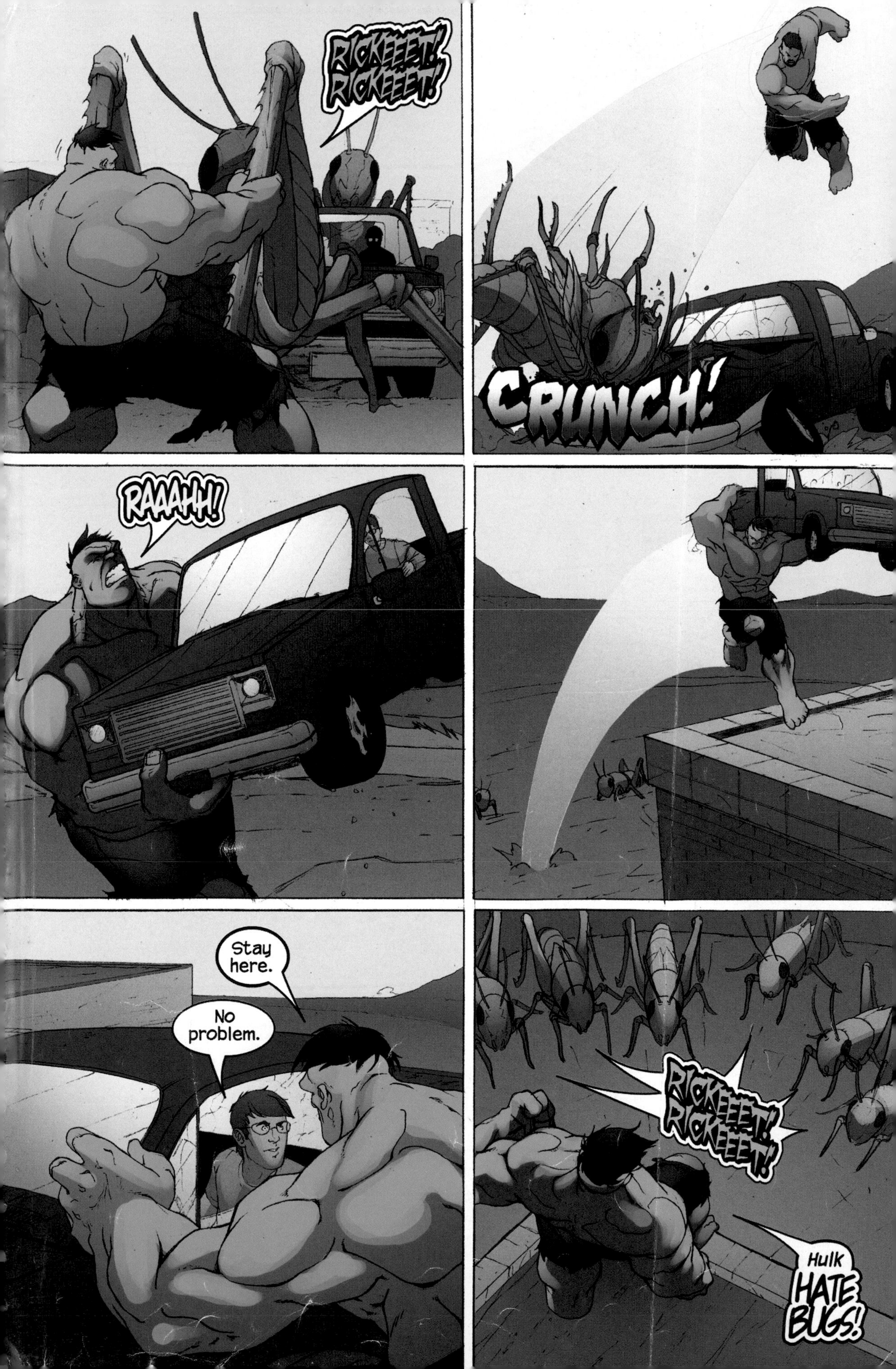
RICKEEEET! RICKEEEET!
CRUNCH!
RAAAHH!
Stay here.
No problem.
RICKEEEET! RICKEEEET!
Hulk HATE BUGS!

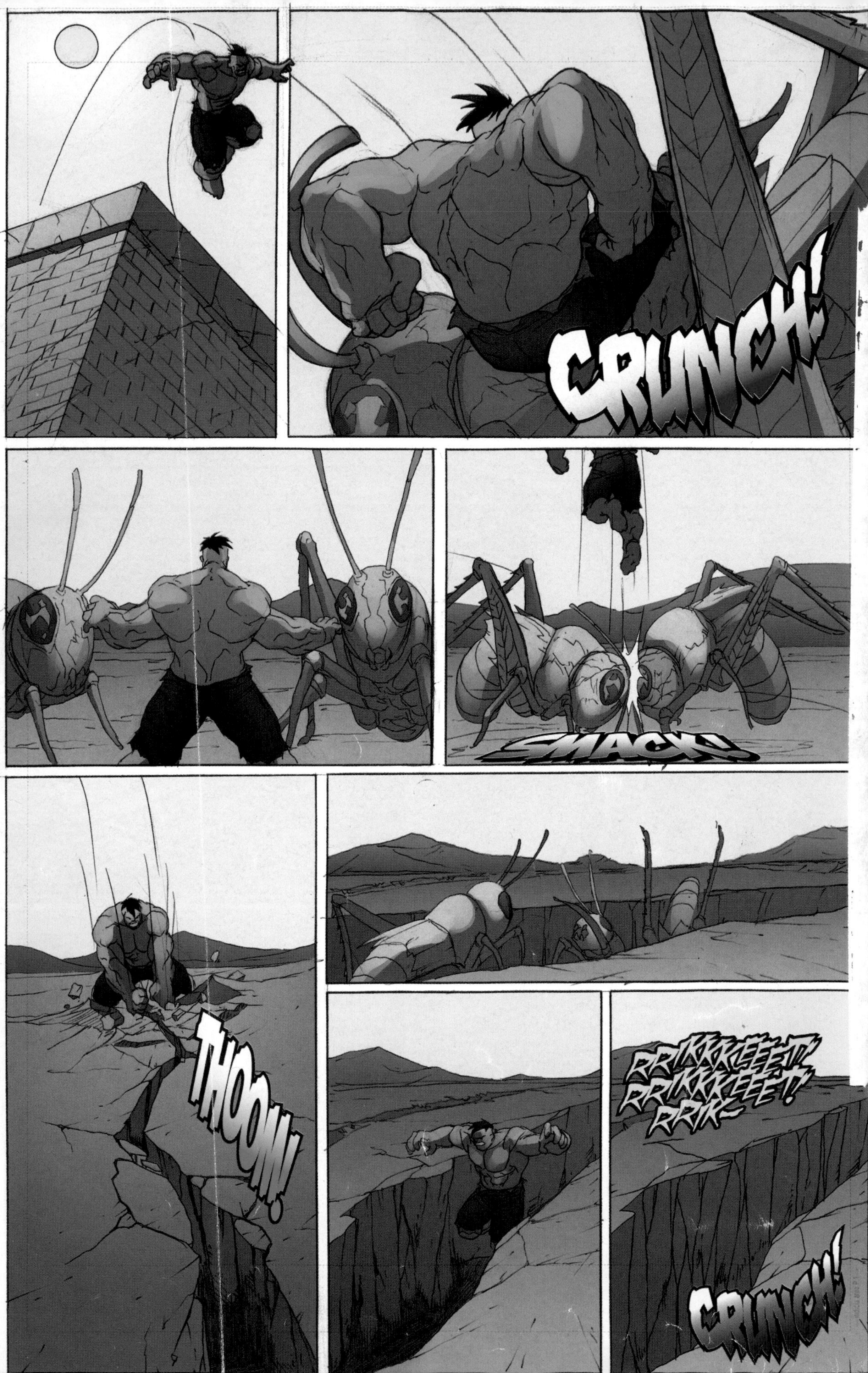
CRUNCH!
SMACK!
THOOM!
RRIKKKREEET!
RRIKKKREEET!
RRIK—
CRUNCH!

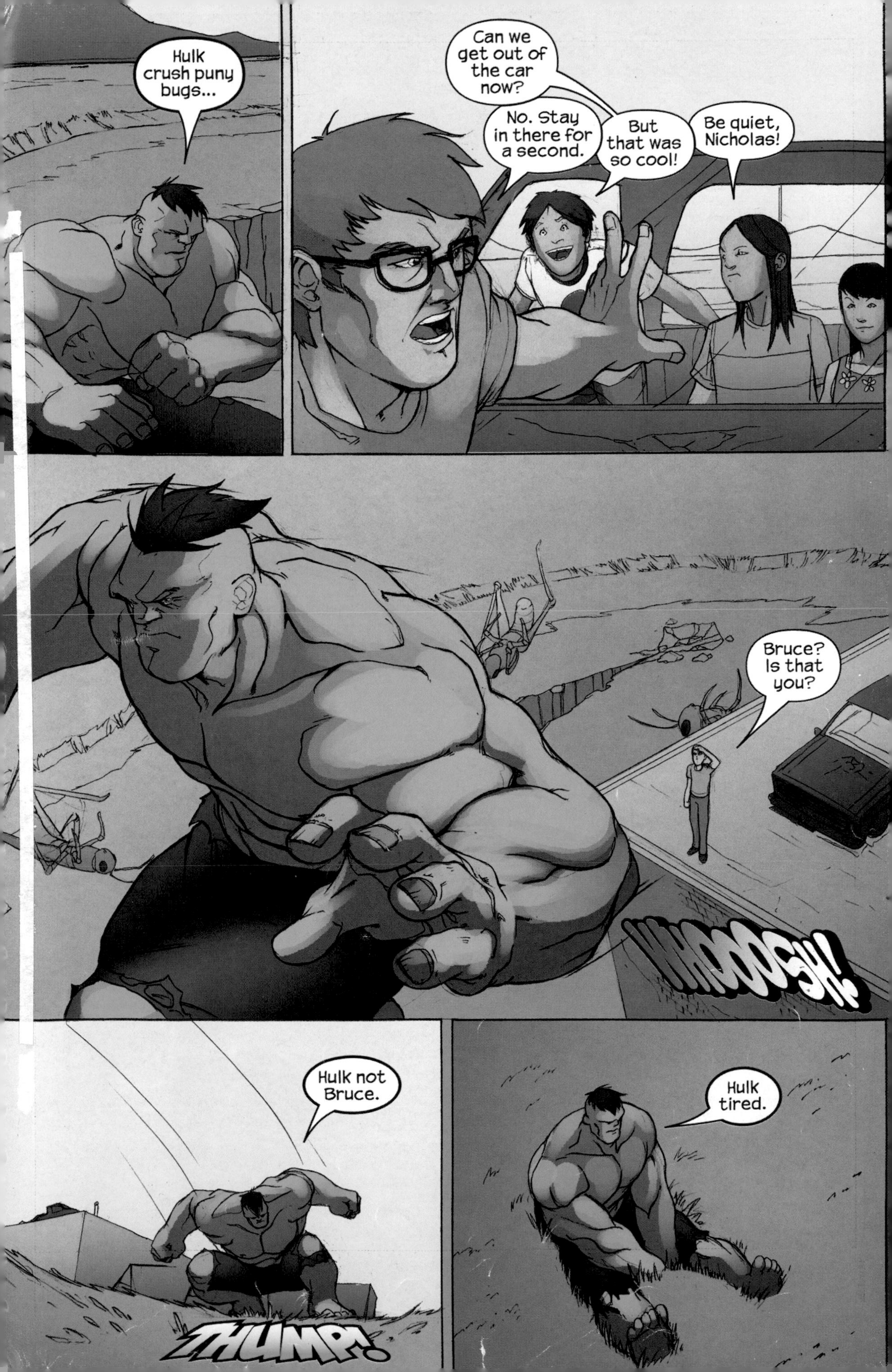

Hulk crush puny bugs...
Can we get out of the car now?
No. Stay in there for a second.
But that was so cool!
Be quiet, Nicholas!
Bruce? Is that you?
WHOOOSH!
Hulk not Bruce.
THUMP!
Hulk tired.

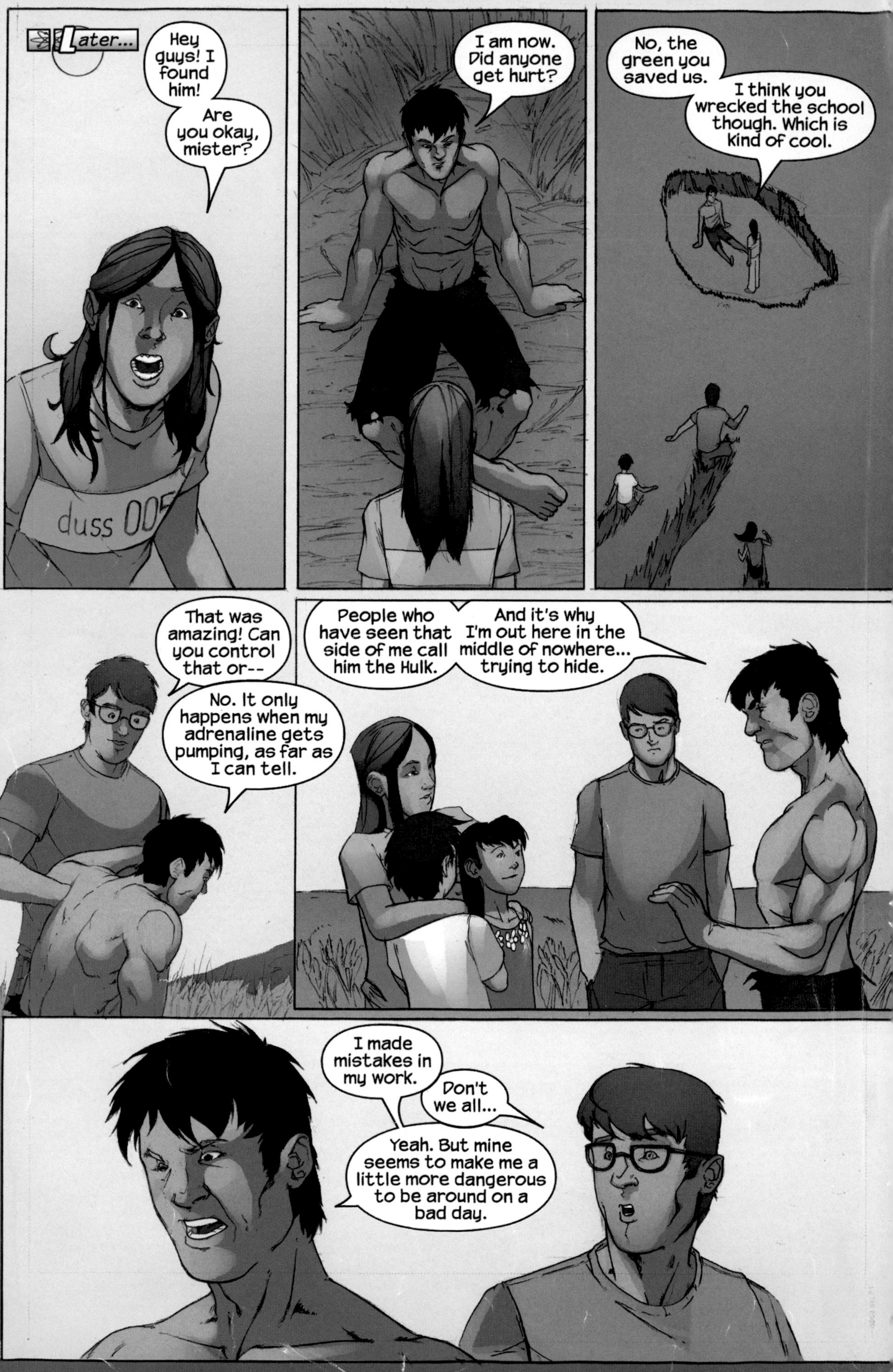
Later...
Hey guys! I found him!
Are you okay, mister?
duss 005
I am now. Did anyone get hurt?
No, the green you saved us.
I think you wrecked the school though. Which is kind of cool.
That was amazing! Can you control that or--
No. It only happens when my adrenaline gets pumping, as far as I can tell.
People who have seen that side of me call him the Hulk.
And it's why I'm out here in the middle of nowhere... trying to hide.
I made mistakes in my work.
Don't we all...
Yeah. But mine seems to make me a little more dangerous to be around on a bad day.

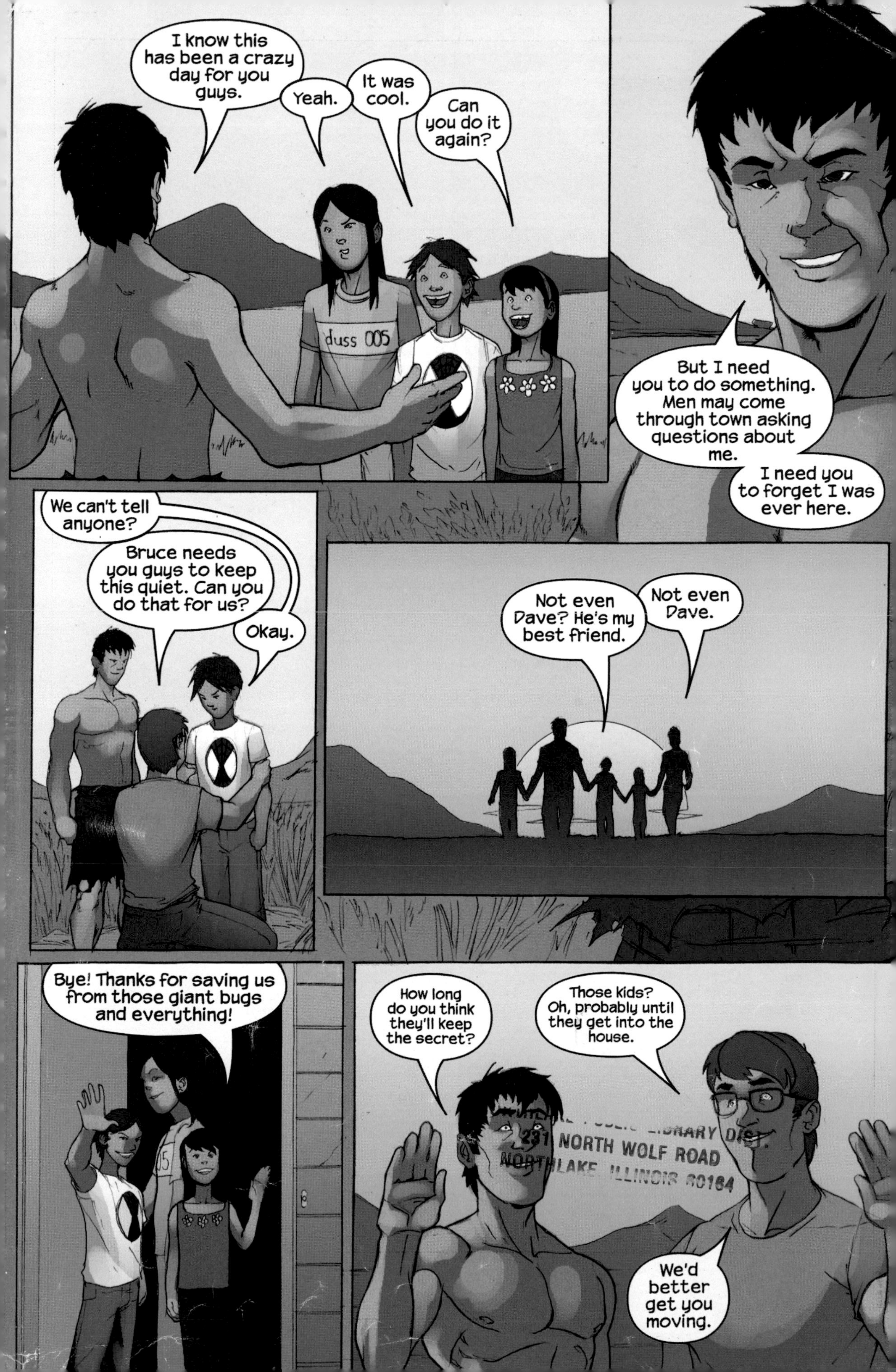
I know this has been a crazy day for you guys.
Yeah.
It was cool.
Can you do it again?
But I need you to do something. Men may come through town asking questions about me.
I need you to forget I was ever here.
We can't tell anyone?
Bruce needs you guys to keep this quiet. Can you do that for us?
Okay.
Not even Dave? He's my best friend.
Not even Dave.
Bye! Thanks for saving us from those giant bugs and everything!
How long do you think they'll keep the secret?
Those kids? Oh, probably until they get into the house.
We'd better get you moving.

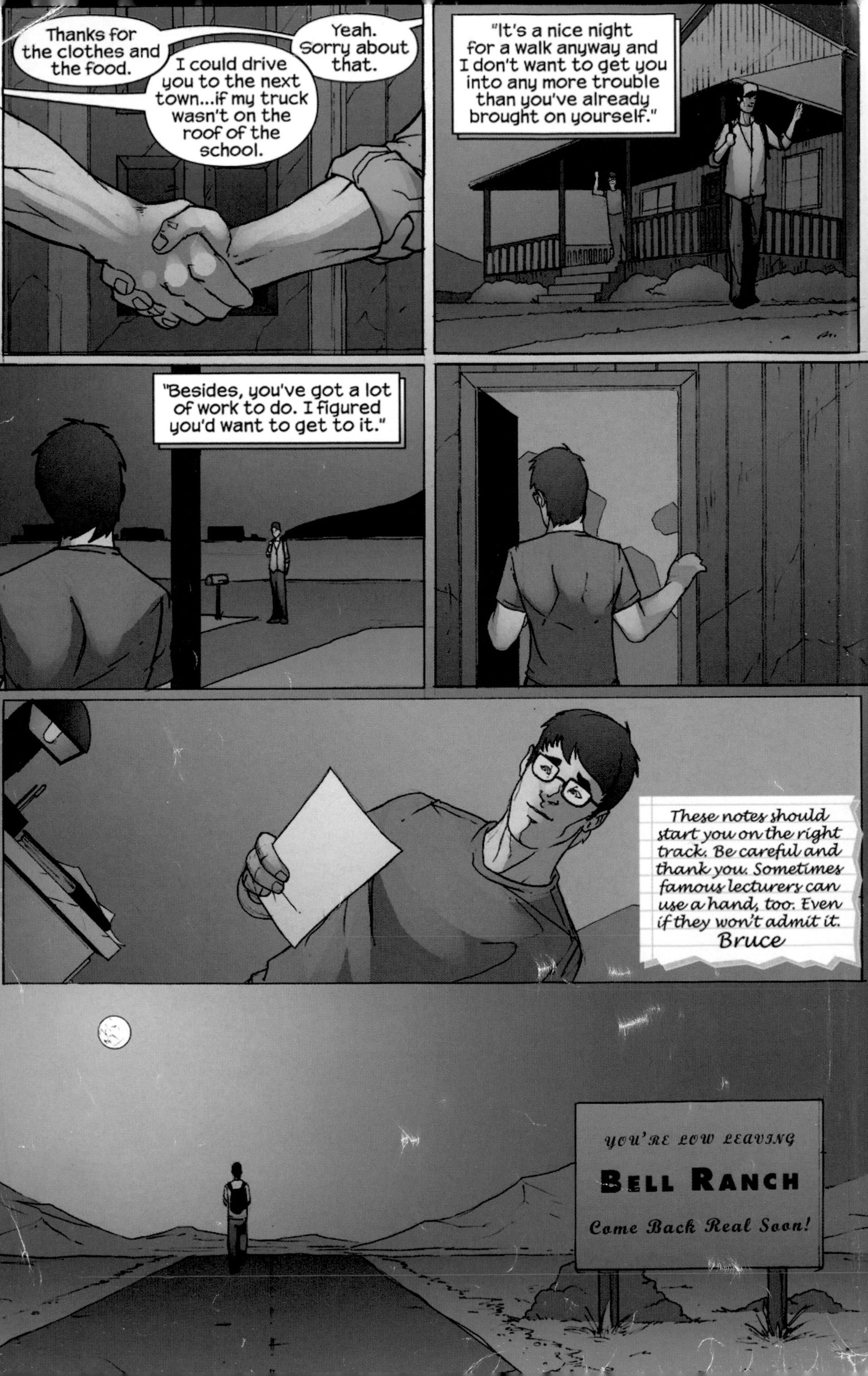
Thanks for the clothes and the food.
Yeah. Sorry about that.
I could drive you to the next town...if my truck wasn't on the roof of the school.
"It's a nice night for a walk anyway and I don't want to get you into any more trouble than you've already brought on yourself."
"Besides, you've got a lot of work to do. I figured you'd want to get to it."
These notes should start you on the right track. Be careful and thank you. Sometimes famous lecturers can use a hand, too. Even if they won't admit it.
Bruce
YOU'RE LOW LEAVING
BELL RANCH
Come Back Real Soon!